Cinderella, Puss in Boots

AND OTHER FAVORITE TALES AS TOLD BY

Charles Perrault

Cinderella, Puss in Boots

AND
OTHER FAVORITE
TALES AS TOLD BY

Charles Perrault

Translated from the French by A. E. Johnson

Harry N. Abrams, Inc., Publishers

Contents

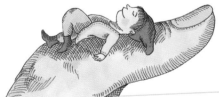

Introduction

Charles Perrault published a collection of eight fairy tales in 1697 entitled *Histoires ou contes du temps passé avec des moralités (Histories or Tales of Long Ago with Morals)*. The work became the most important and popular collection of fairy tales until that of the Grimm Brothers in 1812. These fairy tales were not invented by Perrault; the stories had been passed down through many generations through the spoken word, but Perrault was the first person to write them down in the form which we know today.

Perrault (1628-1703) is best known for the stories in this collection, but he did not begin his career as a writer. Born in Paris, Perrault followed in his father's footsteps and studied law. After completing school, he first worked in the office of his brother, the Receiver General of Paris, and then accepted a job overseeing the construction of royal buildings and palaces for Louis XIV. In 1671, Perrault became a member of the prestigious Académie Française where he explored his interest in writing and literature. Finally, in 1687, he retired to concentrate on his writing.

In the early 1690s Perrault published three verse tales, *Patient Griselda, The Foolish Wishes,* and *Donkeyskin*; a few years later he went on to publish the eight popular fairy tales that are included in this collection: *Little Red Riding Hood, The Fairies, Puss in Boots, Blue Beard, Cinderella, Ricky of the Tuft, The Sleeping Beauty,* and *Little Tom Thumb.* The frontispiece of the original publication listed the alternative title, *Contes de ma mére l'Oye,* or *Tales of Mother Goose,* and these stories have often since come to be known by that name.

Although Perrault's collection is one of the most influential, his versions are not the ones with which we are most familiar. Over the centuries, Perrault's tales have been adapted and changed, and today, many of us do not know the original plots. For example, in Perrault's "Cinderella," the prince hosts two balls instead of one, and Cinderella only loses her glass slipper at the second ball. In "Sleeping Beauty," the beautiful princess is awakened by her prince early in the story. The two are married and have two children, and conflict arises when the prince's mother, an ogress, tries to eat them!

What most differentiates Perrault's versions are the traditional and clever morals included at the end of each tale. These morals are especially helpful in understanding those tales that are more violent. In Perrault's versions, Little Red Riding Hood suffers the same fate as her grandmother, and Blue Beard attempts to do away with his new wife. The violence is not without reason, and the morals offer witty warnings and explanations. When Little Red Riding Hood is eaten by the Wolf, the story's moral warns young women from talking to strangers. When Blue Beard's young wife ventures into the secret chamber that Blue Beard has forbidden her from entering and discovers his horrible secret, the moral reminds us that curiosity nearly cost the young bride her life.

The collection of fairy tales was first published in the name of Perrault's son, Pierre Darmancour. For many years this caused a great deal of debate as to the authorship of the stories, but today that fact is rarely disputed. Pierre was probably nineteen at the time these stories were published, and it is unlikely that a boy his age could have written them. Furthermore, when Perrault first published his three verse tales as a group in 1694, he was greatly criticized for writing childish stories. For a man trying to gain credibility as a writer, this was harsh criticism. Today it is believed that Perrault purposely used his son's name to avoid further embarrassment.

Whatever the actual origin, Charles Perrault's tales provided a humorous, witty, and clever format for the stories that have enchanted readers—and listeners— throughout the centuries, and will continue to do so for years to come.

Little Red Hiding Hood

BY CORINNE CHALMEAU

Once upon a time there was a little village girl, the prettiest that had ever been seen. Her mother doted on her. Her grandmother was even fonder, and made her a little red hood, which became her so well that everyone called her Little Red Riding Hood.

One day her mother baked some cakes. "Go and see how your grandmother is, for I have been told that she is ill," she said. "Take her a cake and this little pot of butter."

Little Red Riding Hood set off at once for her grandmother's house, which was in another village.

On her way through the woods she met old Father Wolf. He would have very much liked to eat her, but dared not do so on account of some woodcutters who were in the forest. He asked her where she was going. The poor child did not know that it was dangerous to stop and talk to a wolf. "I am going to see my grandmother," she said. "I am taking her a cake and a pot of butter that my mother has sent to her."

"Does she live far away?" asked the Wolf.

"Oh, yes," replied Little Red Riding Hood. "Her house is yonder by the mill, which you can see right below there. It is the first house in the village."

"Well now," said the Wolf. "I think I shall go and see her, too. I will go by this path, and you will go by that path, and we will see who gets there first."

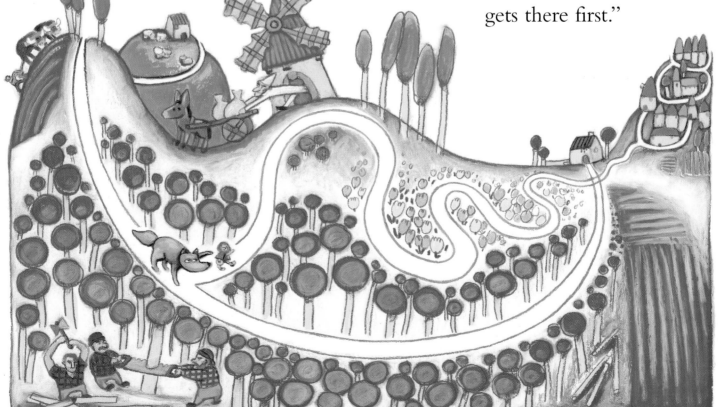

The Wolf set off running with all his
might by the shorter road, and the little girl
continued on her way by the longer road.

As she walked she amused herself by
gathering nuts, running after the
butterflies, and making bouquets of
the wild flowers that she found.

The Wolf was not long in
reaching the grandmother's house.
Knock, knock, he rapped on the door.
"Who is there?"

"It is your granddaughter, Red Riding
Hood," said the Wolf, disguising his voice. "I bring you a cake and a
little pot of butter as a present from my mother."

The grandmother was in bed, not feeling very well. "Pull out the
peg and the latch will fall," she
called.

The Wolf drew out the
peg and the door flew
open. He sprang
upon the poor old

lady and ate her up, for he had been more than three days without food. After that he shut the door, pulled on a nightgown and cap, lay down in the grandmother's bed, and waited for Little Red Riding Hood.

Knock knock, she rapped on the door.

"Who is there?"

Now Little Red Riding Hood, upon hearing the Wolf's gruff voice, was at first frightened, but then assumed that her grandmother had a bad cold. "It is your granddaughter, Red Riding Hood," she replied. "I bring you a cake and a little pot of butter from my mother."

Softening his voice, the Wolf called out to her. "Pull out the peg and the latch will fall," he said.

Little Red Riding Hood did as she was told and the door flew open.

When he saw her enter, the Wolf hid himself in the bed beneath the blankets. "Put the cake and the little pot of butter on the bin," he said. "Then come up on the bed with me."

Little Red Riding Hood took off her cloak, but when she climbed up on the bed she was astonished to see how her grandmother looked in her nightgown.

"Grandmother dear!" she exclaimed. "What big arms you have!"

"The better to embrace you, my child!" the Wolf replied.

"Grandmother dear, what big legs you have!"

"The better to run with, my child!"

"Grandmother dear, what big ears you have!"

"The better to hear with, my child!"

"Grandmother dear, what big eyes you have!"

"The better to see with, my child!"

"Grandmother dear, what big teeth you have!"

"The better to eat you with!"

With these words the wicked Wolf leapt upon Little Red Riding Hood and gobbled her up.

Moral

From this story one learns that children,
Especially young lasses,
Pretty, courteous and well-bred,
Do very wrong to listen to strangers,
For it is not an unheard thing
If the Wolf is thereby provided with his dinner.
I say Wolf, for all wolves
Are not of the same sort;

There is one kind with an amenable disposition
Neither noisy, nor hateful, nor angry,
But tame, obliging and gentle,
Following the young maids
In the streets, even into their homes.
Alas! Who does not know that these gentle wolves
Are of all such creatures the most dangerous!

The Fairies

BY FABIENNE TESSEYDRE

Once upon a time there lived a widow with two daughters. The elder was often mistaken for her mother, so like her was she both in nature and in looks. Parent and child were so disagreeable and arrogant that no one could live with them. The younger girl, who took after her father

in the gentleness and sweetness of her disposition, was also one of the prettiest girls imaginable. The mother doted on the elder daughter—naturally enough, since she resembled her so closely—and disliked the younger one as intensely. She made the latter live in the kitchen and work hard from morning till night.

One of the poor child's many duties was to go twice a day and draw water from a spring a good half-mile away, and to bring it back in a large pitcher. One day when she was at the spring, an old woman came up and begged for a drink.

"Why, certainly, good mother," the pretty lass replied. Rinsing her pitcher, she drew some water from the cleanest part of the spring and handed it to the woman, lifting up the jug so that she might drink more easily.

This old woman was a fairy who had taken the form of a poor village dame to see just how far the girl's good nature would go. "You are so pretty and so polite, that I am determined to bestow a gift upon you," she said when she had finished drinking. "This is the gift I grant you: with every word that you utter there shall fall from your mouth either a flower or a precious stone."

When the girl reached home she was scolded by her mother for being so long in coming back from the spring.

"I am sorry to have been so long, Mother," said the poor child. As she spoke these words there fell from her mouth three roses, three pearls, and three diamonds.

"What is this?" cried her mother. "Did I see pearls and diamonds dropping out of your mouth? What does this mean, dear daughter?" (This was the first time she had ever addressed her daughter affectionately.)

The poor child told the simple tale of what had happened, and in speaking scattered diamonds right and left.

"Really," said her mother. "I must send my own child there. Come here, Fanchon. Look what comes out of your sister's mouth whenever she speaks! Wouldn't you like to be able to do the same? All you have to do is to go and draw some water at the spring, and when a poor woman asks you for a drink, give it to her very nicely."

"Oh, indeed!" replied the ill-mannered girl. "Don't you wish you may see me going there!"

"I tell you that you are to go," said her mother. "Go this instant."

Very sulkily the girl went off, taking with her the best silver pitcher in the house. No sooner had she reached the spring than she saw a lady, magnificently attired, who came toward her from the forest and asked for a drink. This was the same fairy who had appeared to her sister, masquerading now as a princess in order to see how far this girl's ill-nature would carry her.

"Do you think I have come here just to get you a drink?" said the rude girl arrogantly. "I suppose you think I brought this silver pitcher here specially for that purpose? Drink from the spring, if you want to!"

"You are not very polite," said the fairy, displaying no sign of anger.

"Well, in return for your lack of courtesy, I decree that for every word you utter a snake or a toad shall drop out of your mouth."

The moment her mother caught sight of her coming back she cried out, "Well, Daughter?"

"Well, Mother?" replied the rude girl. As she spoke a viper and a toad were spat out of her mouth.

"Gracious heavens!" cried her mother. "What do I see? Her sister is the cause of this, and I will make her pay for it!"

Off she ran to thrash the poor child, but the latter fled away and hid in the forest nearby.

The king's son met her on his way home from hunting and,
noticing how pretty she was, inquired what she was doing all alone
and why she was weeping.

"Alas, sir," she cried. "My mother has driven me from home!"

As she spoke the prince saw four or five pearls and as many
diamonds fall from her mouth. He begged her to tell him how this
came about, and she told him the whole story.

The king's son fell in love with her. He realized the girl's gift was worth more than any dowry that another maiden might bring him, so he took her to the palace of his royal father and married her.

As for the sister, she made herself so hateful that even her mother drove her out of the house. Nowhere could the wretched girl find anyone who would take her in, and at last she lay down in the forest and died.

Moral

Diamonds and golden coins
Can do great things for our spirits.
Kind words, nevertheless,
Have still greater influence
And are in themselves a richer treasure.

Another Moral

Kindness sometimes involves a little trouble
And it takes pains to be considerate,
But sooner or later it has its reward
And often at a moment when it is least expected.

Puss in Boots

BY LIONEL LE NÉOUANIC

A certain miller had three sons. When he died the sole worldly goods that he bequeathed to them were his mill, his ass, and his cat. This little legacy was very quickly divided up among the boys.

The eldest son took the mill, and the second son took the ass. Consequently, all that remained for the youngest son was the cat, and he was more than a little disappointed at receiving such a miserable portion.

"My brothers will be able to get a decent living by joining forces, but for my part, as soon as I have eaten my cat and made a muff out of his skin, I am bound to die of hunger," he said.

These remarks were overheard by Puss, the cat, who pretended not to have been listening. "There is not the least need for you to worry, Master," he said very soberly and seriously. "All you have to do is to give me a pouch, and get a pair of boots made for me so that I can walk in the woods. You will find then that your share is not so bad after all."

Now this cat had often shown himself capable of performing cunning tricks. When catching rats and mice, for example, he would hide himself among the meal and hang downwards by his feet as though he were dead. His new master, therefore, though he did not build too much on what the cat had said, felt some hope of being assisted in his miserable plight.

boots

sack

On receiving the boots he had asked for, Puss happily pulled them on. Then he hung the pouch 'round his neck, and, holding the cords which tied it in front of him with his paws, he sallied forth to a warren where rabbits abounded. Placing some bran and lettuce in the pouch, he stretched himself out and lay as if dead. His plan was to wait until some young rabbit, unlearned in worldly wisdom, should come and rummage in the pouch for the food that he had placed there.

Hardly had he laid himself down when things fell out as he wished. A naive young rabbit went into the pouch, and Master Puss, pulling the cords tight, killed him on the spot. Well satisfied with his capture,

Puss departed to the king's palace. There he demanded an audience, and was ushered upstairs. He entered the royal apartment, and bowed to the king.

"I bring you, Sire, a rabbit from the warren of the Marquis of Carabas (such was the title he invented for his master), which I am bidden to present to you on his behalf," he said.

"Tell your master that I thank him and am pleased by his attention," replied the king.

Another time the cat hid himself in a wheatfield and again kept the mouth of his bag wide open. Two partridges ventured in, and by pulling the cords tight he captured both of them. Off he went and presented them to the king, just as he had done with the rabbit from the warren. His Majesty was as gratified by the brace of partridges, and handed the cat a present for himself.

For two or three months Puss went on in this way, every now and again taking to the king, as a present from his master, some game that he had caught. There came a day when he learned that the king intended to take his daughter, who was the most beautiful princess in the world, for an excursion along the riverbank.

"If you will do as I tell you, your fortune is made," said Puss to his master. "You have only to go and bathe in the river at the spot that I shall point out to you. Leave the rest to me."

The "Marquis of Carabas" had no idea what plan was afoot, but did as the cat had directed. While he was bathing the king drew near, and Puss at once began to cry out at the top of his voice. "Help! Help! The Marquis of Carabas is drowning!"

At these shouts the king put his head out of the carriage window. He recognized the cat who had so often brought him game, and bade his escort go speedily to the help of the Marquis of Carabas.

While they were pulling the poor Marquis out of the river, Puss approached the carriage and explained to the king that while his master was bathing, robbers had come and taken away his clothes, even though he had cried "Stop, thief!" at the top of his voice. As a matter of

fact, the rascal had hidden them under a big stone. The king at once commanded the keepers of his wardrobe to go and select a suit of his finest clothes for the Marquis of Carabas.

The king received the Marquis with many compliments, and as the fine clothes that the latter had just put on set off his good looks (for he was handsome and comely in appearance), the king's daughter found him very much to her liking. Indeed, the Marquis of Carabas had not bestowed more than two or three respectful but sentimental glances upon her when she fell madly in love with him. The king invited him to enter the coach and join the party.

Delighted to see his plan so successfully launched, the cat went on ahead and presently came upon some peasants mowing a field. "Listen, my good fellows," he said. "If you do not tell the king that the field you are mowing belongs to the Marquis of Carabas, you will all be chopped up into little pieces like mincemeat."

In due course the king asked the mowers to whom the field on which they were at work belonged.

"It is the property of the Marquis of Carabas," they all cried with one voice, for the threat from Puss had frightened them.

"You have inherited a fine estate," the king remarked to the Marquis.

"As you see for yourself, Sire," replied the Marquis. "This is a meadow that never fails to yield an abundant crop each year."

Still traveling ahead, the cat came upon some harvesters. "Listen, my good fellows," he said. "If you do not declare that every one of these fields belongs to the Marquis of Carabas, you will all be chopped up into little bits like mincemeat."

The king came by a moment later, and wished to know who was the owner of the fields in sight.

"It is the Marquis of Carabas," cried the harvesters.

At this the king was more pleased than ever with the Marquis.

Preceding the coach on its journey, the cat made the same threat to all whom he met, and the king grew astonished at the great wealth of the Marquis of Carabas.

Finally Master Puss reached a splendid castle that belonged to an ogre. He was the richest ogre that had ever been known, for all the lands through which the king had passed were part of the castle domain.

The cat had taken care to find out who this ogre was and what powers he possessed. He now asked for an interview, declaring that he was unwilling to pass so close to the castle without having the honor of paying his respects to the owner.

The ogre received him as civilly as an ogre could, and bade him to sit down.

"I have been told that you have the power to change yourself into any kind of animal," said Puss. "For example, that you can transform yourself into a lion or an elephant."

"That is perfectly true," said the ogre, curtly. "Just to prove it you shall see me turn into a lion."

Puss was so frightened at seeing a lion before him that he sprang onto the roof—not without difficulty and danger, for his boots were not meant for walking on tiles.

Perceiving presently that the ogre had abandoned his transformation, Puss descended, and owned to having been thoroughly frightened.

TRANSFORMATION!

"I have also been told, but I can scarcely believe it, that you have the further power to take the shape of the smallest animals," he added. "For example, that you can change yourself into a rat or a mouse. I confess that to me it seems quite impossible."

"Impossible?" cried the ogre. "You shall see!" In the same moment he changed himself into a mouse, which began to run about the floor. No sooner did Puss see it than he pounced on it and ate it.

Presently the king came along, and, noticing the ogre's beautiful mansion, desired to visit it. The cat heard the rumble of the coach as it crossed the castle drawbridge and ran out to the courtyard.

"Welcome, your Majesty, to the castle of the Marquis of Carabas!" Puss cried out.

"What is that?" cried the king. "Is this castle also yours, Marquis? Nothing could be finer than this courtyard and the buildings that I see all about. With your permission we will go inside and look around."

The Marquis gave his hand to the young princess and followed the king as he led the way up the staircase. Entering a great hall, they found there a magnificent banquet. This had been prepared by the ogre for some friends who were to pay him a visit that very day. The latter had not dared to enter when they learned that the king was there.

The king was now quite as charmed as his daughter with the excellent qualities of the Marquis of Carabas. The latter was completely

captivated by him. Noting the great wealth of which the Marquis evidently possessed, and having drunk several cups of wine, the king turned to his host.

"It rests with you, Marquis, whether you will be my son-in-law," he said.

The Marquis, bowing very low, accepted the honor the king bestowed upon him. The very same day he married the princess.

Puss became a personage of great importance and gave up hunting mice, except for amusement.

Moral

No matter how great may be the advantages
Of enjoying a rich inheritance,
Coming down from father to son,
Most young people will do well to remember
That industry, knowledge, and a clever mind
Are worth more than mere gifts from others.

Another Moral

If a miller's son, in so short a time,
Can win the heart of a princess,
So that she gazes at him with lovelorn eyes,
Perhaps it is the clothes, the appearance,
    and youthfulness
That are seldom the indifferent means
Of inspiring love!

Blue Beard

BY JERÔME RUILLIER

Once upon a time there was a man who owned splendid town and country houses, gold and silver plates, tapestries and coaches gilt all over. But the poor fellow had a blue beard, and this made him so ugly and frightful that there was not a woman or girl

who did not run away at the sight of him.

Among his neighbors was a lady of high degree who had two beautiful daughters. He asked for the hand of one of these in marriage, leaving it up to their mother to choose which should be bestowed upon him. Both girls raised objections, and his offer was passed from one to the other, neither being able to bring herself to accept a man with a blue beard. Another reason for their distaste was the fact that he had already married several wives, and no one knew what had become of them.

In order that they might become better acquainted, Blue Beard invited the two girls, with their mother and three or four of their best friends, to meet a party of young men from the neighborhood at one of his country houses. Here they spent eight whole days, and throughout their stay there was a constant round of picnics, hunting and fishing expeditions, dances, dinners, and luncheons.

They never slept at all, instead spending all the night playing merry pranks upon each other. In short, everything went so gaily that the younger daughter began to think the master of the house had not so very blue a beard after all, and that he was an exceedingly agreeable man. As soon as the party returned to town their marriage took place.

At the end of the month Blue Beard informed his wife that important business obliged him to make a journey into a distant part of the country, which would occupy at least six weeks. He begged her to amuse herself well during his absence, and suggested that she should invite some of her friends and take them, if she liked, to the country. He was particularly anxious that she should enjoy herself thoroughly.

"Here are the keys to the two large storerooms, and here is the one that locks up the gold and silver plate, which is not in everyday use," he said. "This key belongs to the strong boxes where my gold and silver are kept, this to the caskets containing my jewels, while here you have the master-key which gives admittance to all the apartments. As regards this little key, it is the key to the small room at the end of the long passage on the lower floor. You may open everything, you may go everywhere, but I forbid you to enter this little room. And I forbid you so seriously that if you were indeed to open the door, I should be so angry that I might do anything."

His wife promised to follow these instructions exactly, and, after embracing her, Blue Beard stepped into his coach and went off upon his journey.

Her neighbors and friends did not wait to be invited before coming to call upon her, so great was their eagerness to see the splendors of her house. They had not dared to visit while her husband was there, for his blue beard frightened them. In less than no time there they were, running in and out of the rooms, the closets, and the wardrobes, each of which was finer than the last. Presently they went upstairs to the storerooms, and there they could not admire enough the profusion and magnificence of the tapestries, beds, sofas, cabinets, tables, and stands. There were mirrors in which they could view themselves from head to toe, some with frames of plate glass, others with frames of silver and gilt lacquer, that were the most superb and beautiful things that had ever been seen. They were loud and persistent in their envy of their friend's good fortune. She, on the other hand, derived little amusement from the sight of all these riches, the reason being that she was impatient to go and inspect the little room on the lower floor.

So overcome with curiosity was she that, without reflecting upon the discourtesy of leaving her guests, she ran down a private staircase so recklessly that twice or thrice she nearly broke her neck, and so reached the door of the little room. There she paused for a while, thinking of the prohibition which her husband had made and reflecting on the harm that might come to her as a result of her disobedience. But the temptation was so great that she could not conquer it. Taking the little key, with a trembling hand she opened the door of the room.

At first she saw nothing, for the windows were closed, but after a few moments she realized that the floor was entirely covered with blood, and that in the blood was reflected the dead bodies of several women that hung along the walls. These were all the wives of Blue Beard, whose throats he had cut, one after another. She thought she would die of terror, and the key of the room, which she had just withdrawn from the lock, fell from her hand.

When she had somewhat regained her senses, the bride picked up the key, closed the door, and went up to her chamber to compose herself a little. But this she could not do, for her nerves were too shaken. Noticing that the key of the little room was stained with blood, she wiped it two or three times. But the blood did not go away. She washed it well, and even rubbed it with sand and grit.

The blood remained, for the key was bewitched, and there was no means of cleaning it completely. When the blood was removed from one side, it reappeared on the other.

Blue Beard returned from his journey that very evening. He had received some letters on the way, he said, from which he learned that the business upon which he had set forth had just been concluded to his satisfaction. His wife did everything she could to make it appear that she was delighted by his speedy return.

The next day he demanded the keys. She gave them to him, but with so trembling a hand that he guessed at once what had happened.

"How comes it," he said to her, "that the key of the little room is not with the others?"

"I must have left it upstairs upon my table," she said.

"Do not fail to bring it to me presently," said Blue Beard.

After several delays the key had to be brought. Blue Beard examined it and addressed his wife.

"Why is there blood on this key?"

"I do not know at all," replied the poor woman, paler than death.

"You do not know at all?" exclaimed Blue Beard. "I know well enough. You wanted to enter the little room! Well, Madam, enter it you shal—you shall go and take your place among the ladies you have seen there!"

She threw herself at her husband's feet, asking his pardon with tears and with all the signs of true repentance for her disobedience. She would have softened a rock in her beauty and distress, but Blue Beard had a heart harder than any stone.

"You must die, Madam," he said. "At once."

"Since I must die," she replied, gazing at him with eyes that were wet with tears, "give me a little time to say my prayers."

"I give you one quarter of an hour," replied Blue Beard. "But not a moment longer."

When the poor girl was alone, she summoned her sister. "Sister Anne, go up, I implore you, to the top of the tower, and see if our brothers are not approaching," she said. "They promised they would come and visit me today. If you see them, make signs to them to hasten."

Sister Anne went up to the top of the tower, and the poor unhappy girl cried out to her from time to time. "Anne, Sister Anne, do you see nothing coming?"

"I see nought but dust in the sun and the green grass growing," Sister Anne replied.

Presently, Blue Beard, grasping a great cutlass, cried out at the top of his voice: "Come down quickly, or I shall come upstairs myself."

"Oh please, one moment more," called out his wife. And at the same moment she cried in a whisper, "Anne, Sister Anne, do you see nothing coming?"

"I see nought but dust in the sun and the green grass growing," her sister replied.

"Come down at once, I say," shouted Blue Beard. "Or I will come upstairs myself."

"I am coming," replied his wife. "Anne, Sister Anne, do you see nothing coming?" she called out again.

"I see a great cloud of dust that comes this way," replied Sister Anne.

"Is it our brothers?"

"Alas, Sister, no; it is but a flock of sheep."

"Do you refuse to come down?" roared Blue Beard.

"One little moment more," exclaimed his wife. "Anne, Sister Anne, do you see nothing coming?" she cried once more.

"I see," replied her sister, "two horsemen who come this way, but they are as yet a long way off. Heaven be praised," she exclaimed a moment later. "They are our brothers! I am signaling to them all I can to hasten."

Blue Beard let forth so mighty a shout that the whole house shook. The poor wife went down and cast herself at his feet, all disheveled and in tears.

"That avails you nothing," said Blue Beard. "You must die."

Seizing her by the hair with one hand, and with the other waving the cutlass about, he made as if to cut off her head.

The poor woman, turning toward him and fixing a dying gaze upon him, begged for a brief moment in which to collect her thoughts.

"No! no!" he cried. "Commend your soul to Heaven." He raised his arm.

At this very moment there came a knocking at the gate so loud that Blue Beard stopped short. The gate was opened, and two horsemen dashed in, drawing their swords and riding straight at Blue Beard. The latter recognized them as the brothers of his wife—one of them a dragoon, and the other a musketeer—and fled instantly in an effort to escape. But the two brothers were so close upon

him that they caught him before he could gain the first flight of steps. They plunged their swords through his body and left him dead. The poor woman had not the strength to rise and embrace her brothers.

It was found that Blue Beard had no heirs, and that consequently his wife became mistress of all his wealth. She devoted a portion to arrange a marriage between her Sister Anne and a young gentleman

with whom the latter had been for some time in love, while another portion purchased a captain's commission for each of her brothers. The rest formed a dowry for her own marriage with a very worthy man, who banished from her mind all memory of the evil days she had spent with Blue Beard.

Moral

Curiosity, in spite of its great charms,
Often brings with it serious regrets.
Every day a thousand examples appear.
In spite of a maiden's wishes, it is a fruitless pleasure,
For once satisfied, curiosity offers nothing,
And ever does it cost more dearly.

Another Moral

If one takes a sensible point of view,
And studies this grim story,
He will recognize that this tale
Is one of days long past.
No longer is the husband so terrifying,
Demanding the impossible,
Being both dissatisfied and jealous;
In the presence of his wife he now is gracious enough,
And no matter what color his beard may be
One does not have to guess who is master!

Cinderella

BY FLORENCE PINEL

Once upon a time there was a worthy man whose second wife was the haughtiest, proudest woman who had ever been seen. She had two daughters who possessed their mother's temper and resembled her in every way. Her husband, on the other hand, had a young daughter who was of an exceptionally sweet and gentle nature. She got this from her mother, who had been the nicest of people.

As soon as the wedding was over, the stepmother began to display her bad temper. She could not endure the excellent qualities of this young girl, for they made her own daughters appear more hateful than ever. She thrust upon her all the meanest tasks about the house. It was she who had to clean the plates and the stairs,

and sweep out the rooms of the mistress of the house and her daughters. She slept on a wretched mattress in a garret at the top of the house, while the sisters had rooms with parquet flooring and beds of the most fashionable style, with mirrors in which they could see themselves from head to toe. The poor girl endured everything patiently, not daring to complain to her father. The latter would have scolded her because he was entirely ruled by his wife. When she would finish her work she would sit among the cinders in the corner of the chimney, and it was from this habit that she came to be commonly known as Cinder-clod. The younger of the two sisters, who was not quite so spiteful as the elder, called her Cinderella. But her wretched clothes did not prevent Cinderella from being a hundred times more beautiful than her sisters, for all their resplendent garments.

It happened that the king's son gave a ball, and he invited all persons of high degree. The two young ladies were invited among others. Not a little pleased were they, and the question of what clothes and what mode of dressing the hair would become them best took up all their time. And all this meant fresh trouble for Cinderella, for it was she who went over her sisters' linen and ironed their ruffles. They could talk of nothing else but the fashions in clothes.

"For my part," said the elder, "I shall wear my dress of red velvet with the Honiton lace."

"I have only my everyday petticoat," said the younger. "But to make up for it I shall wear my cloak with the golden flowers and my necklace of diamonds, which is not so bad."

They sent for a good hairdresser to arrange their double-frilled caps, and bought patches at the best shop. They summoned Cinderella and asked her advice, for she had good taste. Cinderella gave them the best possible suggestions and even offered to dress their hair, to which they gladly agreed.

"Cinderella, would you not like to go to the ball?" they said, while she was thus occupied.

"Ah, but you fine young ladies are laughing at me. It would be no place for me."

"That is very true, people would laugh to see a cinder-clod in the ballroom."

Anyone else but Cinderella would have done their hair amiss, but she was so good-natured that she finished them off to perfection. They were so excited that for nearly two days they ate nothing. They broke more than a dozen laces by drawing their corsets tight in order to make their waists more slender, and they were perpetually in front of a mirror.

At last the happy day arrived.
Away they went and Cinderella
watched them as long as she
could keep them in sight. When
she could no longer see them
she began to cry. Her godmother
found her in tears, and asked what
was troubling her.

"I should like—I should like—"
She was crying so bitterly that
she could not finish the
sentence.

"You would like to go to the ball, would you not?" said her godmother, who was a fairy.

"Ah, yes," said Cinderella, sighing.

"Well, well," said her godmother. "Promise to be a good girl and I will arrange everything for you. Now go into the garden and bring me a pumpkin."

Cinderella went at once and gathered the finest that she could find. This she brought to her godmother, wondering how a pumpkin could help in taking her to the ball. Her godmother scooped it out, and when only the rind was left, struck it with her wand. Instantly the pumpkin was changed into a beautiful coach, gilded all over.

Then she went and looked in the mousetrap, where she found six mice all alive. She told

Cinderella to lift the door of the mouse trap a little. As each mouse came out she gave it a tap with her wand, whereupon it was transformed into a fine horse. Soon there was a team of six dappled mouse-gray horses. But the godmother was puzzled about how to provide a coachman.

"I will go and see if there is a rat in the rattrap," said Cinderella. "We could make a coachman of him."

"Quite right," said her godmother. "Go and see."

Cinderella brought in the rattrap, which contained three big rats. The fairy chose one specially on account of his elegant whiskers. As soon as she had touched him he turned into a fat coachman with the finest mustache that was ever seen.

"Now go into the garden and bring me the six lizards which you will find behind the water container," she said.

No sooner had the lizards been brought than the godmother turned them into six lackeys. They at once climbed up behind the coach in their braided uniforms, and hung on there as if they had never done anything else all their lives.

"Well, there you have the means of going to the ball," said the fairy godmother. "Are you satisfied?"

"Oh, yes, but am I to go like this in my ugly clothes?" Cinderella asked.

Her godmother merely touched her with her wand, and on the instant her clothes were changed into garments of gold and silver cloth, bedecked with jewels. After that her godmother gave her a pair of glass slippers.

Thus altered, Cinderella entered the coach. Her godmother bade her not to stay beyond midnight whatever happened, warning her that if she remained at the ball a moment longer, her coach would again become a pumpkin, her horses mice, and her lackeys lizards, while her old clothes would reappear upon her once more. Cinderella promised her godmother that she would not fail to leave the ball before midnight, and away she went, beside herself with delight.

The king's son, when he was told of the arrival of a great princess whom nobody knew, went forth to receive her. He helped her down from the coach, and led her into the hall where the company was assembled. At once there fell a great silence. The dancers stopped and the violins played no more, so rapt was the attention that everybody bestowed upon the superb beauty of the unknown guest. "Oh, how beautiful she is!" everyone whispered.

The king whispered to the queen that it was many a long day since he

had seen anyone so beautiful and charming. All the ladies were eager
to scrutinize her clothes and the dressing of her hair, determined to
copy them on the morrow, provided they could find materials so fine,
and tailors so clever. The king's son placed
her in the seat of honor, and at
once begged the
privilege of being
her partner in a
dance. Such was the
grace with which
she danced that the
admiration of all
was increased.

A magnificent supper was served, but the young prince could eat nothing, so taken was he with watching Cinderella. She went and sat beside her sisters, and bestowed endless attention upon them. She shared with them the oranges and lemons—so hard to come by at this season—that the king had given her. They were greatly astonished, for they did not recognize her.

While they were talking, Cinderella heard the clock strike a quarter to twelve. She at once made a profound curtsey to the company, and departed as quickly as she could. As soon as she was

home again she sought out her godmother and, having thanked her, declared that she wished to go upon the morrow once more to the ball, because the king's son had invited her.

While she was busy telling her godmother all that had happened, her two sisters knocked at the door. Cinderella let them in.

"What a long time you have been in coming!" she declared, rubbing her eyes and stretching herself as if she had only just awakened.

"If you had been at the ball, you would not be feeling weary," said one of the sisters. "There came a most beautiful princess, the most beautiful that has ever been seen, and she bestowed countless attention upon us, and gave us her oranges and lemons."

Cinderella was overjoyed. She asked them the name of the princess, but they replied that no one knew it, and that the king's son was so distressed that he would give anything in the world to know who she was. Cinderella smiled and said

she must have been beautiful indeed.

"Oh, how lucky you are. Could I not manage to see her?" she said. "Oh, please, Javotte, lend me the yellow dress that you wear every day."

"Indeed!" said Javotte. "That is a fine idea. Lend my dress to a grubby cinder-clod like you—you must think me mad!"

Cinderella had expected this refusal. She was in no way upset, for she would have been very greatly embarrassed had her sister been willing to lend the dress.

The next day the two sisters went to the ball, and so did Cinderella, even more splendidly attired than the first time. The king's son was always at her elbow, and paid her endless compliments. The young girl enjoyed herself so much that she forgot her godmother's bidding completely, and when the first stroke of midnight fell upon her ears, she thought it was no later than eleven o'clock.

She rose and fled as nimbly as a fawn. The prince followed, but could not catch her. Cinderella let one of her glass slippers fall, however, and this the prince picked up with tender care.

Inquiries were made of the palace doorkeepers as to whether they had seen a princess go out, but they declared they had seen no one leave except a young girl, very ill-clad, who looked more like a peasant than a young lady.

When Cinderella reached home she was out of breath, without coach, without lackeys, and in her shabby clothes. Nothing remained of all her splendor save one of the little slippers, the fellow to the one she had let fall.

When her two sisters
returned from the ball,
Cinderella asked them if they
had again enjoyed themselves
and if the beautiful lady had
been there. They told her that
she was present, but had fled
away when midnight sounded,
and in such haste that she had
let one of her little glass slippers
fall, the prettiest thing in the
world. They added that the
king's son, who picked it up,
had done nothing but gaze at it
for the rest of the ball. It was
plain that he was deeply in love
with its beautiful owner.

They spoke the truth. A few days
later, the king's son caused a
proclamation to be made by
trumpeters that he would take for his
wife the owner of the foot on which
the slipper would fit. It was first tried
on the princesses, and then on the
duchesses and the whole of the
Court, but in vain. Presently it was
brought to the home of the two

sisters, who did all they could to squeeze a foot into the slipper. This,
however, they could not manage.

Cinderella was looking on and recognized her slipper. "Let me see
if it will not fit me," she cried, laughingly.

Her sisters burst out laughing and began to gibe at her, but the
prince's man looked closely at Cinderella. Observing that she was very
beautiful, he declared that the claim was quite a fair one, and that his

orders were to try the slipper on every maiden. He bade Cinderella sit down, and on putting the slipper to her little foot he perceived that the latter slid in without trouble and was molded to its shape like wax.

Great was the astonishment of the two sisters at this, and greater still when Cinderella drew from her pocket the other little slipper. This she likewise slipped on. At that very moment her godmother appeared on the scene. She gave a tap with her wand to Cinderella's clothes, and transformed them into a dress even more magnificent than her previous ones.

The two sisters recognized her as the beautiful person whom they had seen at the ball, and threw themselves at her feet, begging her pardon for all the ill-treatment she had suffered at their hands. Cinderella embraced them, declaring that she pardoned them with all her heart and bade them to love her well in future. She was taken to the palace of the young prince in all her new array. He found her more beautiful than ever, and was married to her a few days afterward. Cinderella was as good as she was beautiful. She set aside apartments in the palace for her two sisters, and married them the very same day to two gentlemen of high rank about the Court.

Moral

Beauty in a maid is an extraordinary treasure;
One never tires of admiring it.
But what we mean by graciousness
Is beyond price and still more precious.
It was this that her godmother gave Cinderella,
Teaching her to become a queen.
(So the moral of this story goes.)
Lasses, this is a better gift than looks so fair
For winning over a heart successfully.
Graciousness is the true gift of the Fairies.
Without it, one can do nothing;
With it, one can do all!

Another Moral

It is surely a great advantage
To have spirit and courage,
Good breeding and common sense,
And other qualities of this sort,
Which are the gifts of Heaven!
You will do well to own these;
But for success, they may well be in vain
If, as a final gift, one has not
The blessing of godfather or godmother.

Ricky of the Tuft

BY STÉPHAN LAPLANCHE

Once upon a time there was a queen who bore a son so ugly and misshapen that for some time it was doubtful if he would have human form at all. A fairy who was present at his birth promised that he should have plenty of brains, and added that by virtue of the gift

which she had just bestowed upon him, he would be able to impart to the person whom he should love best the same degree of intelligence that he possessed himself.

This somewhat consoled the poor queen, who was greatly disappointed at having brought into the world such a hideous brat. And indeed, no sooner did the child begin to speak than his sayings proved to be full of shrewdness, and all he did was somehow so clever that he charmed everyone.

I forgot to mention that when he was born he had a little tuft of hair upon his head. For this reason he was called Ricky of the Tuft, Ricky being his family name.

Some seven or eight years later the queen of a neighboring kingdom gave birth to twin daughters. The first one to come into the world was more beautiful than the dawn, and the queen was so overjoyed that it was feared her great excitement might do her some harm. The same fairy who had assisted at the birth of Ricky of the Tuft was present, and in order to moderate the ecstasy of the queen, she declared that this little princess would have no sense at all, and would be as stupid as she was beautiful.

The queen was deeply mortified, and a moment or two later her chagrin became greater still, for the second daughter proved to be extremely ugly.

"Do not be distressed, Madam," said the fairy. "Your daughter shall be recompensed in another way. She shall have so much good sense that her lack of beauty will scarcely be noticed."

"May Heaven grant it!" said the queen. "But is there no means by which the elder, who is so beautiful, can be endowed with some intelligence?"

"In the matter of brains I can do nothing for her, Madam," said the fairy. "But, as regards beauty, I can do a great deal. As there is nothing I would not do to please you, I will bestow upon her the power of making beautiful any person who shall greatly please her."

As the two princesses grew up their perfections increased, and everywhere the beauty of the elder and the wit of the younger were the subject of common talk. It was equally true that their defects also increased as they became older. The younger grew uglier every minute, and the elder became more stupid daily. Either she answered nothing at all when spoken to, or she replied with some idiotic remark. She was so awkward that she could not set four china vases on the mantelpiece without breaking one of them, nor drink a glass of water without spilling half of it over her clothes.

Now although the elder girl possessed the great advantage that beauty always confers upon youth, she was nevertheless outshone in almost all company by her younger sister. At first everyone gathered around the beauty to see and admire her, but very soon they were all attracted by the graceful and easy conversation of the clever one. In a very short time the elder girl would be left entirely alone, while everybody clustered 'round her sister.

The elder princess was not so stupid that she was not aware of this, and she would willingly have surrendered all her beauty for half her sister's cleverness. Sometimes she was ready to die of grief, for the queen, though a sensible woman, could not refrain from occasionally reproaching her about her stupidity.

One day when the princess retired to the woods to bemoan her misfortune, she saw an ugly little man of very disagreeable appearance, but clad in magnificent attire, approaching her. This was the young prince, Ricky of the Tuft. He had fallen in love with her portrait, which was everywhere to be seen, and had left his father's kingdom in order to have the pleasure of seeing and talking to her.

Delighted to meet her thus alone, he approached with every mark of respect and politeness. But while he paid her the usual compliments, he noticed that she was deep in melancholy.

"I cannot understand, Madam, how anyone with your beauty can be so sad as you appear," he said. "I can boast of having seen many fair ladies, and I declare that none of them could compare in beauty with you."

"It is very kind of you to say

so, sir," answered the princess and stopped there, for she was at a loss of what to say further.

"Beauty is of such great advantage that everything else can be disregarded," said Ricky. "I do not see that the possessor of it can have anything much to grieve about."

"I would rather be as plain as you are and have some sense, than be as beautiful as I am and at the same time stupid," the princess replied.

"Nothing more clearly displays good sense, Madam, than a belief that one is not possessed of it. It follows, therefore, that the more one has, the more one fears it to be wanting."

"I am not sure about that," said the princess. "But I know only too well that I am very stupid, and this is the reason of the misery that is nearly killing me."

"If that is all that troubles you, Madam, I can easily put an end to your suffering."

"How will you manage that?" said the princess.

"I am able, Madam, to bestow as much good sense as it is possible to possess on the person whom I love the most," said Ricky of the Tuft. "You are that person, and it therefore rests with you to decide whether you will acquire so much intelligence. The only condition is that you shall consent to marry me."

The princess was dumbfounded, and remained silent.

"I can see that this suggestion perplexes you, and I am not surprised," said Ricky. "I will give you a whole year to make up your mind to it."

The princess had so little sense, and at the same time desired it so ardently, that she persuaded herself that the end of the year would never come. So she accepted the offer that had been made

to her. No sooner had she given her word to Ricky that she would marry him within one year from that very day, than she felt a complete change come over her. She found herself able to say all that she wished with the greatest ease, and to say it in an elegant, finished, and natural manner. She at once engaged Ricky in a brilliant and lengthy conversation, holding her own so well that Ricky feared he had given her a larger share of sense than he had retained for himself.

On her return to the palace, amazement reigned throughout the court at such a sudden and extraordinary change. Whereas formerly they had been accustomed to hear the princess make silly, pert remarks, they now heard her express herself sensibly and very wittily. The entire court was overjoyed. The only person not too pleased was the younger sister, for now that she no longer had the advantage over the elder in wit, she seemed nothing but a little fright in comparison. The king himself even took his elder daughter's advice, and several times held his councils in her apartment.

The news of this change spread abroad, and the princes of the neighboring kingdoms made many attempts to captivate the princess. Almost all asked for her hand in marriage, but she found none with enough sense, and so she listened to all without promising herself to any.

At last came one who was so powerful, so rich, so witty, and so handsome that the princess could not help being somewhat attracted to him. Her father noticed this, and told her she could make her own choice of a husband; she had only to declare herself. Now the more sense one has, the more difficult it is to make up one's mind in an affair of this kind. After thanking her father, therefore, the princess asked for a little time to think it over. In order to ponder quietly what she had better do, she went to walk in a wood—the very one, as it happened, where she had encountered Ricky of the Tuft.

While she walked, deep in thought, she heard a thudding sound beneath her feet, as though many people were running busily to and fro. Listening more attentively, she heard voices. "Bring me that pot," said one. "Put some wood on that fire!" said another.

At that moment the ground opened, and the princess saw below what appeared to be a large kitchen full of cooks and scullions, and all the train of attendants involved in the preparation of a great banquet. A gang of some twenty or thirty spit-turners emerged and took their positions around a very long table in a path in the wood. They all wore their cook's

caps on one side, and, with their basting implements in their hands, they kept time together as they worked to the lilt of a melodious song.

The princess was astonished by this spectacle and asked for whom their work was being done.

"For Prince Ricky of the Tuft, Madam," said the foreman of the gang. "His wedding is tomorrow."

At this the princess was more surprised than ever. In a flash she remembered that it was a year to the very day since she had promised to marry Prince Ricky of the Tuft, and was taken aback by the recollection. The reason she had forgotten was that when she had made the promise she was still without sense; with the acquisition of the intelligence that the prince had bestowed upon her, all memory of her former stupidities had been blotted out. She had not gone another thirty paces when Ricky of the Tuft appeared before her, gallant and resplendent, like a prince upon his wedding day.

"As you see, Madam, I keep my word to the minute," he said. "I do not doubt that you have come to keep yours and give me your hand to make me the happiest of men."

"I will be frank with you," replied the princess. "I have not yet made up my mind on that point, and I am afraid I shall never be able to make the decision you desire."

"You astonish me, Madam," said Ricky of the Tuft.

"I can believe it," said the princess. "Undoubtedly, if I had to deal with a clown, or a man who lacked good sense, I should feel myself very awkwardly situated. 'A princess must keep her word,' he would

say, 'and you must marry me because you promised to!' But I am speaking to a man of the world, of the greatest good sense, and I am sure that he will listen to reason. As you are aware, I could not make up my mind to marry you even when I was entirely without sense. How can you expect that today, possessing the intelligence you bestowed on me, which makes me still more difficult to please than formerly, I

should make a decision which I could not make then? If you wished so much to marry me, you were very wrong to relieve me of my stupidity and to let me see more clearly than I did."

"If a man who lacked good sense would be justified, as you have just said, in reproaching you for breaking your word, why do you expect, Madam, that I should act differently when the happiness of my whole life is at stake?" replied Ricky of the Tuft. "Is it reasonable that people who have sense should be treated worse than those who have none? Would you maintain that for a moment—you, who so markedly have sense and desired so ardently to have it? But, pardon me, let us get to the facts. With the exception of my ugliness, is there anything about me that displeases you? Are you dissatisfied with my

breeding, my brains, my disposition, or my manners?"

"In no way," replied the princess. "I like exceedingly all that you have displayed of the qualities you mention."

"In that case, happiness will be mine," said Ricky of the Tuft. "For it lies in your power to make me the most attractive of men."

"How can that be done?" asked the princess.

"It will happen of itself if you love me well enough to wish that it be so," replied Ricky of the Tuft. "To remove your doubts, Madam, let me tell you that the same fairy who on the day of my birth bestowed upon me the power of endowing with intelligence the woman of my choice, gave to you also the power of endowing with beauty the man whom you should love, and on whom you should wish to confer this favor."

"If that is so," said the princess, "I wish with all my heart that you may become the handsomest and most attractive prince in the world, and I give you without reserve the blessing that is mine to bestow."

No sooner had the princess uttered these words than Ricky of the Tuft appeared before her eyes as the handsomest, most graceful, and most attractive man that she had ever set her eyes upon.

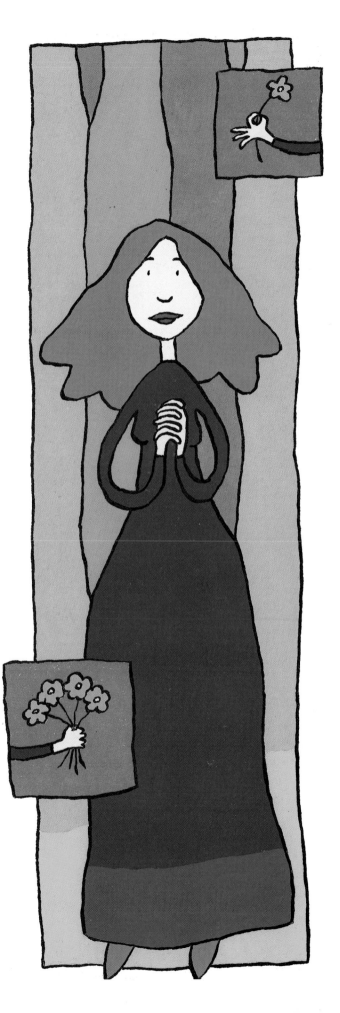

Some people assert that this was not the work of fairy enchantment, but that love alone had brought about the transformation. They say that the princess, as she mused upon her lover's constancy, his good sense, and his many admirable qualities of heart and head, grew blind to the deformity of his body and the ugliness of his face; that his humpback seemed no more than was natural in a man who could make the courtliest of bows, and that the dreadful limp that had formerly distressed her now seemed nothing more than a certain bashfulness and charming

deference of manner. They say
further that she found his eyes
shone all the brighter for their
squint, and that this defect in
them was to her but a sign of
passionate love; while his great
red nose she found manly and
heroic.

Whatever the truth may be,
the princess promised to
marry him on the
spot, provided
only that he
could obtain
the consent
of her royal
father. The
king knew
Ricky of the
Tuft to be a prince
both wise and witty,
and, on learning of his
daughter's regard for him,
he accepted him with pleasure
as a son-in-law.

The wedding took place upon the morrow, just as Ricky of the Tuft had foreseen, and in accordance with the arrangements he had long ago planned and brought about.

Moral

*That which you see written here
Is less a story than the truth itself.
Everything is beautiful in the one we love
And all that we love has beauty.*

Another Moral

*In one whom Nature has blessed with a
    beautiful disposition,
And whose living portrait has that
Which Art can never match;
All these gifts have less effect
In touching a heart
Than a single invisible charm
Which love alone knows how to discover.*

The Sleeping Beauty

BY FLORENCE LANGLOIS

Once upon a time there lived a king and queen who were grieved, more grieved than words can tell, because they had no children. They traveled the waters of every country, made vows and pilgrimages, and did everything that could be done, but without result. At last, however, the queen found that her wishes were fulfilled, and in due course she gave birth to a daughter.

A grand christening was held, and all the fairies
that could be found in the realm (they numbered
seven in all) were invited to be godmothers to
the little princess. This was done so that by
means of the gifts each would bestow
upon her (in accordance with the fairy
custom of those days), the princess might be
endowed with every imaginable perfection.

When the christening ceremony was over, all
the company returned to the king's palace where a great
banquet was held in honor of the fairies. Places were laid for them in
magnificent style, and a solid gold casket containing a spoon, fork, and
knife of fine gold, set with diamonds and rubies, was placed before
each. But just as all were sitting down to the table, an aged fairy was
seen to enter, whom no one had thought to invite—the reason being
that for more than fifty years she had never left the tower in which
she lived, and people had supposed her to be dead or bewitched.

By the king's order a place was laid for her, but it was impossible to give her a golden casket like the others, for only seven had been made for the seven fairies. The old creature believed that she was intentionally slighted, and muttered threats under her breath.

She was overheard by one of the young fairies who was seated nearby. The latter, guessing that some mischievous gift might be bestowed upon the little princess, hid behind the tapestry as soon as the company left the table. Her intention was to be the last to speak, and so to have the power of counteracting, as far as possible, any evil the old fairy might do.

Presently the fairies began to bestow their gifts upon the princess.

The youngest ordained that she should be the most beautiful person in the world; the next, that she should have the temper of an angel; the third, that she should do everything with wonderful grace; the fourth, that she should dance to perfection; the fifth, that she should sing like a nightingale; and the sixth, that she should play every kind of music with the utmost skill.

It was now the turn of the aged fairy. Shaking her head in token of spite rather than of infirmity, she declared that the princess should prick her hand with a spindle and die of it.

A shudder ran through the company at this terrible gift. All eyes were filled with tears.

But at this moment the young fairy stepped forth from behind the tapestry.

"Take comfort your Majesties," she cried in a loud voice. "Your daughter shall not die. My power, it is true, is not enough to undo all that my aged kinswoman has decreed; the princess will indeed prick her hand with a spindle. But instead of dying, she shall merely fall into a profound slumber that will last a hundred years. At the end of that time a king's son shall come to awaken her."

The king, in an attempt to avert the unhappy doom pronounced by the old fairy, at once published an edict forbidding all persons, under pain of death, to use a spinning wheel or keep a spindle in the house.

At the end of sixteen years the king and queen happened one day

to be away. The princess was running about the castle. Going upstairs from room to room, she came at length to a garret at the top of a tower, where an old serving woman sat alone with her distaff, spinning. This good woman had never heard of the king's proclamation forbidding the use of spinning wheels.

"What are you doing, my good woman?" asked the princess.

"I am spinning, my pretty child," replied the dame, not knowing who she was.

"Oh, what fun!" rejoined the princess. "How do you do it? Let me try and see if I can do it equally well."

Partly because she was too hasty, partly because she was a little heedless, and partly because the fairy decree had ordained it, no sooner had she seized the spindle than she pricked her hand and fell down in a swoon.

In great alarm the good dame cried out for help. People came running from every quarter of the castle to the princess. They threw water on her face, chafed her with their hands, and rubbed her temples. But nothing would restore her.

Then the king, who had been brought upstairs by the commotion, remembered the fairy prophecy. Feeling certain that what had happened was inevitable since the fairies had decreed it, he gave orders that the princess should be placed in the finest apartment in the palace, upon a bed embroidered in gold and silver.

You would have thought her an angel, so fair was she to behold. The trance had not taken away the lovely color of her complexion. Her cheeks were delicately flushed, her lips like coral. Her eyes, indeed, were closed, but her gentle breathing could be heard, and it was therefore plain that she was not dead. The king

commanded that she should be left to sleep in peace until the hour of her awakening should come.

When the accident happened to the princess, the good fairy who had saved her life by condemning her to sleep a hundred years was in a far off kingdom, twelve thousand leagues away. She was instantly warned of it, however, by a little dwarf who had a pair of seven-league boots, which are boots that enable one to cover seven leagues at a single step. The fairy set off at once, and within an hour, her chariot of fire, drawn by dragons, was seen approaching.

The king helped her down from her chariot, and she approved of all that he had done. Being blessed with great powers of foresight, she thought to herself that when the princess came to be awakened, she would be much distressed to find herself all alone in the old castle.

She touched with her wand everybody (except the king and queen) who was in the castle—governesses, maids of honor, ladies-in-waiting, gentlemen, officers, stewards, cooks, scullions, errand boys, guards, porters, pages, and footmen. She touched likewise all the horses in the stables and their grooms, the big mastiffs in the courtyard, and little Puff, the pet dog of the princess, who was lying on the bed beside his mistress. The moment she touched them they each fell asleep, to awaken only at the same moment as their mistress. Thus they

would always be ready with their service whenever she should require it. The very spits before the fire, loaded with partridges and pheasants, subsided into slumber, and the fire did as well. All was done in a moment, for the fairy did not take long to complete her work.

Then the king and queen kissed their dear child without waking her and left the castle. Proclamations forbidding any approach to it were issued, but these warnings were not needed, for within a quarter of an hour there grew up all around the park so vast a

quantity of trees big and small, with interlacing brambles and thorns, that neither man nor beast could penetrate them. The tops of the castle towers alone could be seen, but only from a distance. Thus did the fairy's magic ensure that the princess, during the time of her slumber, should have nothing to fear from prying eyes.

At the end of a hundred years, the throne had passed to another family from that of the sleeping princess. One day the current king's son chanced to go hunting in the way of the princess's castle, and seeing in the

distance some towers in the midst of a large and
dense forest, he asked what they were. His
attendants told him in reply the various
stories they had heard. Some said it
was an old castle haunted by ghosts,
others that all the witches of the
neighborhood held their revels there.
Their favorite tale was that in the
castle lived an ogre who carried
around all the children whom he
could catch. At the castle he
devoured them at his leisure,
and, since he was the only
person who could force a
passage through the woods,
nobody had been able to
pursue him.

While the prince was
wondering what to
believe, an old peasant
told of another tale.

"Your Highness,"
he said. "More than
fifty years ago I
heard my father say
that in this castle lies
a princess, the most

beautiful that has ever been seen. It is her doom to sleep there for a hundred years and then to be awakened by a king's son, for whose coming she waits."

This story excited the young prince. He immediately jumped to the conclusion that it was up to him to see the adventure through, and, impelled alike by the wish for love and glory, he resolved to set about it on the spot.

Hardly had he taken a step toward the wood when the tall trees, the brambles, and the thorns, separated themselves and made a path for him. The prince turned in the direction of the castle, and saw it at the end of a long avenue. He entered this avenue, and was surprised to notice that the trees closed up again as soon as he had passed, so that none of his entourage was able to follow him. A young and gallant prince is always brave, however, so he continued on his way and presently reached a large outer courtyard.

The sight that now met his gaze filled him with an icy fear. The silence of the place was dreadful, and death seemed all about him. The reclining figures of men and animals all had the appearance of being lifeless, until the prince perceived by the pimply noses and ruddy faces of the porters that they merely slept. It was plain, too, from their glasses, in which were still some dregs of wine, that they had fallen asleep while drinking.

The prince made his way into an even greater courtyard paved with marble. Mounting the staircase, he entered the guardroom. Here the guards were lined up on either side in two ranks, their muskets on their shoulders, snoring their hardest.

Through several apartments crowded with ladies- and gentlemen-in-waiting, some seated, some standing, but all asleep, he pushed on, and so came at last to a chamber, which was decked all over with gold. There he encountered the most beautiful sight he had ever seen.

Reclining upon a bed, the curtains of which on every side were drawn back, was a princess of seemingly sixteen summers, whose radiant beauty had an almost unearthly luster.

Trembling in his admiration, the prince drew near and went on his knees beside her. At the same moment, the hour of disenchantment having come, the princess awoke and bestowed upon him a look more tender than a first glance might seem to warrant.

"Is it you, dear prince?" she said. "You have been long in coming!"

Charmed by these words, and especially by the manner in which they were said, the prince scarcely knew how to express his delight and gratification. He declared that he loved her better than he loved himself. His words were faltering, but they pleased the more for that. The less there is of eloquence, the more there is of love.

Her embarrassment was less than his, but that is not to be wondered at, since she had had time to think of what she would say to him. It seems (although the story says nothing about it) that the good fairy had beguiled her long slumber with pleasant dreams. To be brief,

after four hours of talking they had not succeeded in uttering one half of the things they had to say to each other.

Now the whole palace had awakened with the princess. Everyone went about his business, and since they were not all in love, they presently began to feel mortally hungry. The lady-in-waiting, who was suffering like the rest, at length lost patience and in a loud voice called out to the princess that supper was served.

The princess was already fully dressed, and in a most magnificent style. As he helped her to rise, the prince refrained from telling her that her clothes, with the straight collar that she wore, were like those to which his grandmother had been accustomed. And in truth, they in no way detracted from her beauty.

They passed into an apartment hung with mirrors, and were there served supper by the stewards of the household, while the fiddles and oboes played some old music—they played it remarkably well, considering they had not played at all for just upon a hundred years. A little later, when supper was over, the chaplain married the prince and the princess in the castle chapel. In due course, attended by the courtiers in waiting, the couple retired to rest.

They slept but little, however. The princess, indeed, had not much

need of sleep, and as soon as morning came, the prince took his leave of her. He returned to the city and told his father, who was awaiting him with some anxiety, that he had gotten lost while hunting in the forest, but had obtained some black bread and cheese from a charcoal burner, in whose hovel he had passed the night. His royal father, being of an easygoing nature, believed the tale, but his mother was not so easily fooled. She noticed that he now went hunting every day, and that he always had an excuse handy when he had slept two or three nights from home. She felt certain, therefore, that he was involved in some love affair.

Two whole years passed since
the marriage of the prince
and princess, and during that
time they had two children.
The first, a daughter, was
called Dawn, while the
second, a boy, was named Day,
because he seemed even more
beautiful than his sister.

Many a time the queen told her son that he ought to settle down
in life. She tried in this way to make him confide in her, but he did
not dare trust her with his secret. Despite the affection he bore her,
he was afraid of his mother, for she came from a race of ogres, and
the king had only married her for her wealth. It was whispered at the

court that she had ogrish instincts, and that when little children were near her, she had the greatest difficulty in the world keeping herself from pouncing on them.

No wonder the prince was reluctant to say a word.

But at the end of two years the king died, and the prince found himself upon the throne. He then made public announcement of his marriage, and went in state to fetch his royal consort from her castle. With her two children beside her she made a triumphal entry into the capital of her husband's realm.

Some time afterwards the king declared war on his neighbor, the Emperor Cantalabutte. He appointed the queen-mother as regent in his absence, and entrusted his wife and children to her care.

He expected to be away at war for the whole of the summer, and as soon as he was gone, the queen-mother sent her daughter-in-law and the two children to a country mansion in the forest. This she did so she might be able to gratify her horrible longings more easily. A few days later she went there herself, and in the evening summoned the chief steward.

"For my dinner tomorrow, I will eat little Dawn," she told him.

"Oh, Madam!" exclaimed the steward.

"That is my will," said the queen, speaking in the tones of an ogress who longs for raw meat. "You will serve her with piquant sauce," she added.

The poor man, seeing plainly that it was useless to trifle with an ogress, took his knife and went up to little Dawn's chamber. She was at that time four years old, and when she came running with a smile to greet him, flinging her arms 'round his neck and coaxing him to give her some sweets, he burst into tears and let the knife fall from his hand.

Presently he went down to the yard behind the house and slaughtered a young lamb. For this he made so delicious a sauce that his mistress declared she had never eaten anything so good. At the same time the steward carried little Dawn to his wife, and bade the latter to hide her in the quarters they had below the yard.

Eight days later the wicked queen summoned her steward again.

"For my supper, I will eat little Day," she announced.

The steward made no answer, determined to trick her

as he had done previously. He
went in search of little Day,
whom he found with a play
sword in his hand making brave
passes—though he was but three
years old—at a big monkey. He
carried the child off to his wife,
who stowed him away in hiding
with little Dawn. To the ogress
the steward served, in place of
Day, a young kid so tender that
she found it delicious.

So far, so good. But there
came an evening when this evil
queen again addressed the
steward.

"I have a mind to eat the
queen with the same sauce as
you served with her children,"
she said.

This time the poor steward despaired at the idea of being able to practice another deception. The young queen was twenty years old, not counting the hundred years she had been asleep. Her skin, though white and beautiful, had become a little tough, and what animal could he possibly find that would correspond to her? He made up his mind that to save his own life he must kill the young queen, and went upstairs to her apartment determined to do the deed once and for all.

Goading himself into a rage, he drew his knife, entered the young queen's chamber, and informed her respectfully of the command that he had received from the queen-mother.

"Do it! Do it!" she cried, baring her neck to him. "Carry out the order you have been given! Then once more I shall see my children, my poor children that I loved so much!"

Nothing had been said to her when the children were stolen away, and she believed them to be dead. The poor steward was overcome by compassion. "No, no, Madam," he declared. "You shall not die, but you shall certainly see your children again. That will be in my quarters, where I have hidden them. I shall make the queen eat a young deer in place of you, and thus trick her once more."

Without more ado he led her to his quarters and, leaving her there to embrace and weep over her children, proceeded to cook a hind with such art that the queen-mother ate it for her supper with as much appetite as if it had indeed been the young queen.

The queen-mother felt well satisfied with her cruel deeds and planned to tell the king, on his return, that savage wolves had devoured his wife and children. It was her habit, however, to prowl often about the courts and alleys of the mansion in the hope of scenting raw meat, and one evening she heard the little boy Day crying in a basement cellar. The child was weeping because his mother had threatened to whip him for some naughtiness, and she heard at the same time the voice of Dawn begging forgiveness for her brother.

The ogress recognized the voices of the queen and her children and was enraged to find that she had been tricked. The next morning, in tones so frightening that all trembled, she ordered a huge vat to be brought into the middle of the courtyard. This she filled with vipers and toads,

with snakes and serpents of every kind, intending to cast into it the queen and her children, and the steward and his wife and serving-girl. By her command, these were brought forward with their hands tied behind their backs.

The queen-mother's attendants were preparing to cast them into the vat when into the courtyard rode the king! Nobody had expected him so soon, but he had traveled as fast as possible. Filled with amazement, he demanded to know what this horrible spectacle meant. None dared tell him, and at that moment the ogress, enraged at what

confronted her, threw herself head first into the vat, and was devoured instantly by the hideous creatures she had placed in it.

The king could not be but sorry, for after all she was his mother, but it was not long before he found ample consolation in his beautiful wife and children.

Moral

To wait a bit in choosing a husband
Rich, courteous, genteel, and kind,
That is understandable enough.
But to wait a hundred years, and all the time asleep,
Not many maidens would be found with such patience.
This story, however, seems to prove
That marriage bonds,
Even though they be delayed, are none the less blissful,
And that one loses nothing by waiting.
But maidens yearn for the wedding joys
With so much ardor
That I have neither strength nor the heart
To preach this moral to them.

Little Tom Thumb

BY EMMANUELLE HOUDART

Once upon a time there lived a woodcutter and his wife who had seven children, all boys. The eldest was only ten years old, and the youngest was seven. People were astonished that the woodcutter had had so many children in so short a time, but the reason was that his wife delighted in children, and never had less than two at a time.

They were very poor and their seven
children were a great burden on them,
for none of them was yet able to earn
his own living. They were troubled also
because the youngest was very delicate
and could not speak a word. They
mistook for stupidity what was in reality
a mark of good sense.

The youngest boy was very little. At
his birth he was scarcely bigger than a
man's thumb, and he was called in
consequence "Little Tom Thumb." The
poor child was the scapegoat of the
family, and got the blame for everything.
All the same, he was the sharpest and
shrewdest of the brothers, and if he
spoke but little he listened much.

There came a very bad year and the
famine was so great that these poor

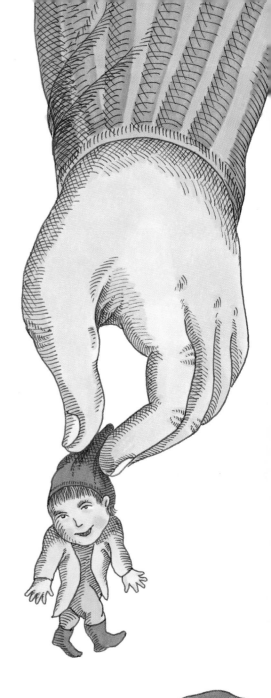

people resolved to get rid of their family. One evening, after the children had gone to bed, the woodcutter was sitting in the chimney corner with his wife. His heart was heavy with sorrow. "It must be plain enough to you that we can no longer feed our children," he said. "I cannot see them die of hunger before my eyes, and I have made up my mind to take them tomorrow to the forest and leave them there. It will be easy enough to manage, for while they are amusing themselves by collecting sticks and branches, we have only to disappear without them seeing us."

"Ah!" cried the woodcutter's wife. "Do you mean to say you are capable of letting your own children get lost?"

In vain did her husband remind her of their terrible poverty, but she could not agree. She was poor, but she was their mother. In the end, however, reflecting what a grief it would be to see them die of hunger, she consented to the plan and went weeping to bed.

Little Tom Thumb had heard all that was said. Having discovered, when in bed, that serious talk was going on, he had risen quietly and had slipped under his father's stool in order to listen without being seen. He went back to bed but did not sleep a wink for the rest

of the night, thinking over what he had better do. In the morning he rose very early and went to the edge of a brook. There he filled his pockets with little white pebbles and quickly came home again. Soon the family all set out, and Little Tom Thumb said not a word to his brothers of what he knew.

They went into a forest, which was so dense that when only ten paces apart they could not see each other. The woodcutter set about his work, and the children began to collect twigs. Presently the father and mother, seeing them busy at their task, edged gradually away and then hurried off in haste along a little narrow footpath.

When the children found they were alone, they began to cry and call out with all their might. Little Tom Thumb let them cry, confident that they would get back home again, for on the way he had dropped the little white stones that he carried in his pocket all along the path.

"Do not be afraid, brothers," he said. "Our parents have left us here, but I will take you home again. Just follow me."

They fell in line behind him, and he led them straight to their house by the same path they had taken to the forest. At first they dared

not go in, but placed themselves against the door, where they could hear everything their father and mother were saying.

Now the woodcutter and his wife had no sooner reached their home than the lord of the manor sent them a sum of ten crowns that he had owed them for a long time, and of which they had given up hope of ever receiving. The woodcutter sent his wife off to the butcher at once, and, as it was such a long time since they had had anything to eat, she bought three times as much meat as a supper for two required. When they found themselves once more at the table, the woodcutter's wife began to lament.

"Alas! where are our poor children now?" she said. "They could make a good meal of what we have over. Mind you, William, it was you who wished to lose them. I declared over and over again that we should not leave them. What are they doing now in that forest? Merciful heavens, perhaps the wolves have already eaten them! A monster you must be to lose your children in this way!"

The woodcutter claimed he too was as grieved as she, but what was done was done.

"Alas!" cried the woodcutter's wife, bursting into tears. "Where are my children now, my poor children?"

She said it so loud that the children at the door heard it plainly. "Here we are! Here we are!" they all called out together.

She rushed to open the door for them. "How glad I am to see you again, dear children!" she exclaimed as she embraced them. "You must be very tired and very hungry. And you, Peterkin, how muddy you are—come and let me wash you!"

Peterkin was her eldest son. She loved him more than all the others because he was inclined to be red-headed, and she herself was rather red. They sat down at the table and ate with an appetite their parents were happy to see. They all talked at once and recounted the fears they had felt in the forest.

The good souls were delighted to have their children with them again, and the pleasure continued as long as the ten crowns lasted. But when the money was all spent they relapsed into their former sadness. They again resolved to lose the children and to lead them much farther away than they had done the first time, so as to do the job thoroughly. But though they were careful not to speak openly about it, their conversation did not escape Little Tom Thumb, who made up his mind to get out of the situation as he had done on the former occasion.

But though he got up early to go and collect his little stones, he found the door of the house doubly locked, and he could not carry out his plan.

He could not think what to do until the woodcutter's wife gave them each a piece of bread for breakfast. Then it occurred to him to use the bread in place of the stones and to throw crumbs along the path. He tucked the bread tight in his pocket.

Their parents led them into the thickest and darkest part of the forest, and as soon as they were there, slipped away by a side path and left them. This did not much trouble Little Tom Thumb, for he believed he could easily find the way back by means of the bread

that he had scattered wherever he walked. But to his dismay, he could not find a single crumb. The birds had come along and eaten it all.

They were in sore trouble now, for with every step they strayed farther away, and became more and more entangled in the forest. Night came and a terrific wind arose, which filled them with dreadful alarm. On every side they seemed to hear nothing but the howling of wolves that were coming to eat them up. They dared not speak or move. In addition, it began to rain so heavily that they were soaked to the skin. At every step they tripped and fell on the wet ground, getting up again covered with mud.

Little Tom Thumb climbed to the top of a tree in an effort to see something. Looking all about him he saw, far away on the other side of the forest, a little light like that of a candle. He got down from the tree and was terribly disappointed to find that when he was on the ground he could see nothing at all.

After they had walked some distance in the direction of the light, however, he caught a glimpse of it again as they were nearing the edge of the forest. At last they reached the house where the light was burning, but not without much anxiety, for every time they had to go down into a hollow, they lost sight of it again.

They knocked at the door, and a
good dame opened it to them. She
asked them what they wanted. Little
Tom Thumb explained that they
were poor children who had lost
their way in the forest and begged
her, for pity's sake, to give them a
night's lodging.

Noticing what young and tender
children they all were, the woman began to cry. "Alas, my poor little
dears!" she said. "You do not know the place you have come to!
Have you not heard that this is the house of an ogre who eats
little children?"

"Alas, Madam!" answered Little Tom Thumb, trembling like all the rest of his brothers. "What shall we do? One thing is very certain. If you do not take us in, the wolves of the forest will devour us this very night, and that being so we should prefer to be eaten by your husband. Perhaps he will take pity on us, if you will plead for us."

The ogre's wife, thinking she might be able to hide them from her husband until the next morning, allowed them to come in and placed them to warm near a huge fire, where a whole sheep was cooking on the spit for the ogre's supper. Just as they were beginning to get warm they heard two or three great bangs at the door. The ogre had returned. His wife hid them quickly under the bed and ran to let him in.

The first thing the ogre did was to ask whether supper was ready and the wine opened. Then, without ado, he sat down at the table. Blood was still dripping from the sheep, but it seemed all the better to him for that. He sniffed right and left, declaring that he could smell fresh flesh.

"Indeed!" said his wife. "It must be the calf which I have just dressed that you smell."

"*I smell fresh flesh*, I tell you," shouted the ogre, eyeing his wife askance. "There is something going on here that I do not understand."

With these words he got up from the table and went straight to the bed. One after another he dragged the children out from under it.

"Aha!" he said. "So this is the way you deceive me, wicked woman that you are! I have a great mind to eat you, too! It is lucky for you that you are old and tough! I am expecting three ogre friends of mine to pay me a visit in the next few days, and here is a tasty dish that will come in just nicely for them!"

The poor children threw themselves on their knees, imploring for mercy, but they had to deal with the most cruel of all ogres. Far from pitying them, he was already devouring them with his eyes and repeating to his wife that when cooked with a good sauce they would make the most dainty morsels.

Off he went to get a large knife, which he sharpened on a large stone in his left hand as he drew near the poor children.

He had already seized one of them when his wife called out to him. "What do you want to do it now for?" she said. "Will it not be time enough tomorrow?"

"Hold your tongue," replied the ogre. "They will be all the more tender tonight."

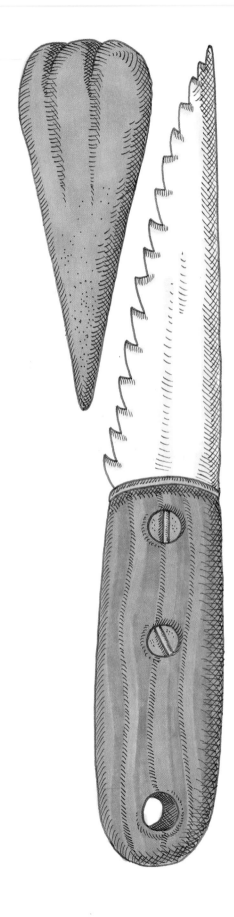

"But you have such a lot of meat," declared his wife. "Look, there are a calf, two sheep, and half a pig."

"You are right," said the ogre. "Give them a good supper to fatten them up, and take them to bed."

The good woman was overjoyed and brought them a splendid supper, but the poor little wretches were so filled with fright they could not eat.

As for the ogre, he went back to his drinking, very pleased to have such good entertainment for his friends. He drank a dozen cups more than usual, and was obliged to go off to bed early, for the wine had gone somewhat to his head.

Now the ogre had seven daughters who as yet were only children. These little ogresses all had the most lovely complexions, for, like their father, they ate fresh meat. But they had little round gray eyes, crooked noses, and very large mouths, with long and exceedingly sharp teeth, set far apart. They were not so very wicked at present, but they showed great promise, for already they were in the habit of killing little children to suck their blood. They had gone to

bed early, and were all seven in a great bed, each with a crown of gold upon her head. In the same room there was another bed, equally large. Into this the ogre's wife put the seven little boys, and then went to sleep herself beside her husband.

Little Tom Thumb was fearful lest the ogre should suddenly regret that he had not cut the throats of himself and his brothers the evening before. Having noticed that the ogre's daughters all had golden crowns upon their heads, he got up in the middle of the night and softly placed his own cap and those of his brothers on their heads. Before doing so, he carefully removed the crowns of gold, putting them on his own and his brothers' heads.   In this way, if the ogre were to feel like slaughtering them that night, he would mistake the girls for the boys, and vice versa.

Things worked out just as he had anticipated. The ogre, waking up at midnight, regretted that he had postponed until the morning what he could have done overnight. Jumping briskly out of bed, he seized his knife. "Now then, let us see how the little rascals are; we will not make the same mistake twice!" he cried.

He groped his way up to his daughters' room and approached the bed in which the seven little boys lay. All were sleeping with the exception of Little Tom Thumb, who was numb with fear when he

felt the ogre's hand, after it touched the head of each of his brothers, reach his own.

"Upon my word," said the ogre, as he felt the golden crowns. "A nice job I was going to make of it! It is very evident that I drank a little too much last night!"

Forthwith he went to the bed where his daughters were and there he felt the little boys' caps. "Aha, here are the little scamps," he cried. "Now for a smart bit of work!"

With these words, and without a moment's hesitation, he cut the throats of his seven daughters. Well satisfied with his work, he went back to bed beside his wife.

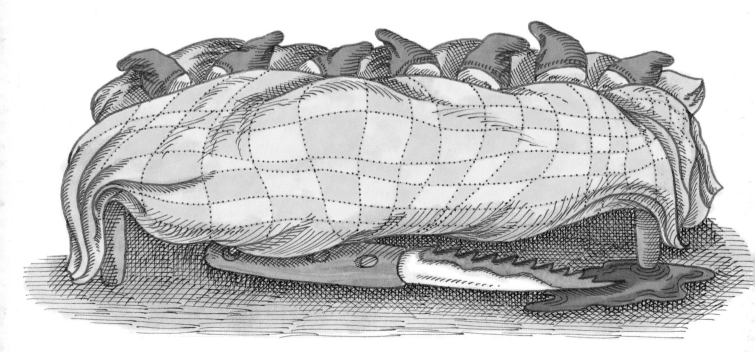

No sooner did Little Tom Thumb hear the ogre snoring than he woke up his brothers and bid them to dress quickly and follow him. They crept quietly down to the garden, and jumped from the wall. All through the night they ran in haste and terror, without the slightest idea of where they were going.

When the ogre woke up he turned to his wife. "Go upstairs and dress those little rascals who were here last night," he said.

The ogre's wife was astonished at her husband's kindness, never doubting that he meant her to go and put on their clothes. She went upstairs, and was horrified to discover her seven daughters bathed in blood, with their throats cut. She fell at once into a

swoon, which is the way of most women in similar circumstances.

The ogre, thinking his wife was very long in carrying out his orders, went up to help her and was no less astounded than his wife at the terrible spectacle that confronted him. "What is this I have done?" he exclaimed. "I will be revenged on the wretches, and quickly, too!"

He threw a jugful of water over his wife's face, and having brought her 'round, ordered her to fetch his seven-league boots, so that he might overtake the children. He set off for the countryside and strode far and wide until he came to the road along which the poor children were traveling. They were not more than a few yards from their home when they saw the ogre striding from hilltop to hilltop, and stepping over rivers as though they were merely tiny streams.

Little Tom Thumb noticed near at hand a cave in some rocks. In this he hid his brothers and himself, while continuing to keep a watchful eye upon the movements of the ogre.

Now the ogre was feeling very tired after so much fruitless marching (for seven-league boots are very fatiguing to their wearer), and felt like taking a little rest. As it happened, he went and sat down on the very rock beneath which the little boys were hiding. Overcome

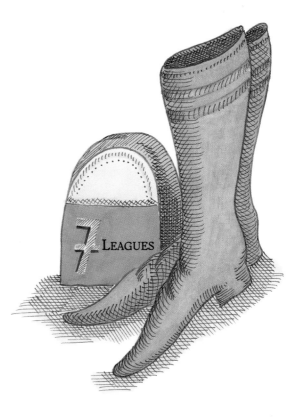

with weariness, he had not sat there long before he fell asleep and began to snore so terribly that the poor children were as frightened as when he had held his great knife to their throats. Little Tom Thumb was not so alarmed. He told his brothers to flee at once to their parents while the ogre was still sleeping soundly, and not to worry about him. They took his advice and ran quickly home.

Little Tom Thumb now approached the ogre and gently pulled off his boots, which he at once donned himself. The boots were very heavy and very large, but being enchanted boots, they had the ability of growing larger or smaller according to the leg they had to suit. Consequently, they always fit as though they had been made for the wearer.

Little Tom Thumb went straight to the ogre's house, where he found the ogre's wife weeping over her murdered daughters.

"Your husband is in great danger, for he has been captured by a gang of thieves, and they have sworn to kill him if he does not hand over all his gold and silver," said Little Tom Thumb. "Just as they had the dagger at his throat, he caught sight of me and begged me to come to you and thus rescue him from his terrible plight. You are to give me everything of value that he possesses without keeping a thing, or else he will be slain without mercy. As the matter is urgent, he wished me to wear his

seven-league boots to save time, and also to prove to you that I am no impostor."

The ogre's wife, in great alarm, immediately gave him all that she had, for although this was an ogre who devoured little children, he was by no means a bad husband. Little Tom Thumb, laden with all the ogre's wealth, forthwith returned to his father's house where he was received with great joy.

Many people do not agree about this last adventure, and pretend that Little Tom Thumb never committed this theft from the ogre, and only took the seven-league boots, about which he had no regrets since they were only used by the ogre for catching little children. These folks assert that they are in a position to know, having been

guests at the woodcutter's cottage. They further say that when Little Tom Thumb had put on the ogre's boots, he went off to the Court where he knew there was great anxiety concerning the result of a battle that was being fought by an army two hundred leagues away. They say that he went to the king and undertook, if desired, to bring news of the army before the day was out, and that the king promised him a large sum of money if he could carry out his project.

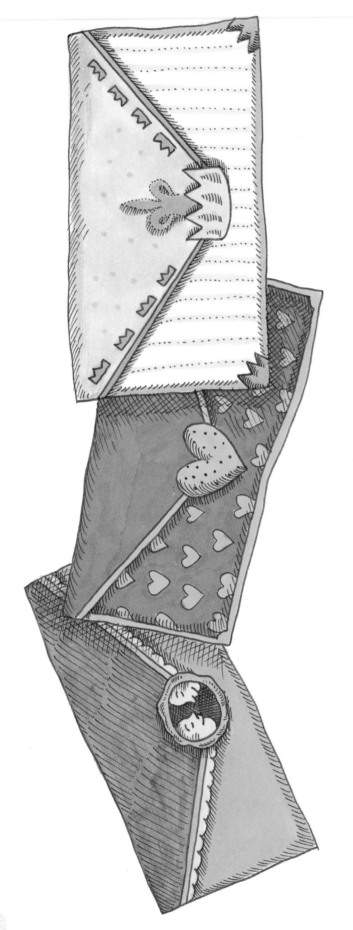

Little Tom Thumb brought news that very night, and, this first errand having brought him into notice, he made as much money as he wished. For not only did the king pay him handsomely to carry orders to the army, but many ladies at the Court gave him anything he asked to bring them news of their lovers, and this was his greatest source of income. He was occasionally entrusted by wives with letters to their husbands, but they paid him so badly, and this branch of the business brought him in so little, that he did not even bother to reckon what he made from it.

After acting as courier for some time, and amassing great wealth thereby, Little Tom Thumb returned to his father's house, and was there greeted with the greatest joy imaginable. He made all his

family comfortable, buying newly created positions at Court for his father and brothers. In this way he set them all up, not forgetting at the same time to look well after himself.

Moral

Having many children seldom brings unhappiness,
Especially if they are attractive, well-bred, and strong.
But if one is sickly or is slow of wit,
How often is he despised, jeered at, and scorned!
Although sometimes it is this oddest one
Who brings good fortune to all the family!

Editor, English-language edition: Lia Ronnen

Library of Congress Cataloging-in-Publication Data

Perrault, Charles, 1628-1703
    [Contes des fées. English. Selections]
    Cinderella, Puss in Boots, and other favorite tales / as told by Charles Perrault.
            p.   cm.
        Contents: Little Red Riding Hood / illustrated by Corinne Chalmeau—The fairies /
illustrated by Fabienne Fesseydre—Puss in Boots / illustrated by Lionel le Néouanic—Blue
Beard / illustrated by Jérôme Ruillier—Cinderella / illustrated by Florence Pinel—Ricky of
the Tuft / illustrated by Stéphan Laplanche—Sleeping Beauty in the woods / illustrated by
Florence Langlois—Little Tom Thumb / illustrated by Emmanuelle Houdart.
        ISBN 0-8109-4014-0
        1. Fairy tales—France.   [1. Fairy tales. 2. Folklore—France.]
    I. Title
    PZ8.P426Ci   1999c
    [398.2'0944]—dc21   98-53961

ABRAMS Harry N. Abrams, Inc.
        100 Fifth Avenue
        New York, N.Y. 10011
        www.abramsbooks.com